ZIPPITY

Heather Grovet Series Book Two

READY TO RIDE SERIES

Pacific Press® Publishing Association
Nampa, Idaho
Oshawa, Ontario, Canada
www.pacificpress.com

Copyright 2007 by
Pacific Press® Publishing Association
Printed in the United States of America
All rights reserved

Book design by Gerald Lee Monks
Cover photo/illustration © Mary Bausman

Additional copies of this book are available by calling
toll-free 1-800-765-6955 or by
visiting http://www.adventistbookcenter.com.

Library of Congress Cataloging-in-Publication Data

Grovet, Heather, 1963-
Zippitty do dah : trusting God in troubles great and
small / Heather Grovet.
    p. cm. — (Ready to ride ; bk. 2)
Summary: Along with her friends Kendra and Megan,
Ruth-Ann and her mischievious pony Zipper prepare
for a jumping show where she learns what is truly
important in life.
ISBN 13: 978-0-8163-2165-0
ISBN 10: 0–8163–2165-5
[1. Ponies. 2. Friendship. 3. Christian life.] I. Title.

PZ7.G931825Zip 2007
dc22   2006052760

07 08 09 10 11 • 5 4 3 2 1

Also by Heather Grovet

Ready to Ride Series

A Perfect Star

Good as Gold

More titles coming!

Other books by Heather Grovet

Beanie: The Horse That Wasn't a Horse

Marvelous Mark and His No-good Dog

Petunia the Ugly Pug

Prince: The Persnickety Pony That Didn't Like Grown-ups

Prince Prances Again

Sarah Lee and a Mule Named Maybe

What's Wrong With Rusty?

Dedication

To my horse loving friend Ruth and her handsome Morgan, Alex!

Contents

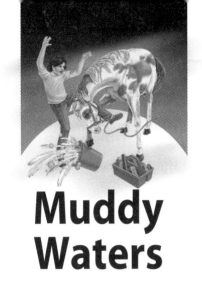

Muddy
Waters

Ruth-Ann Chow, Kendra Rawling, and Megan Lewis stood inside the Lewis family's barn, bathing their ponies. "I had no idea how much fun it would be to wash a horse!" Ruth-Ann exclaimed. She reached over with a soapy sponge and scrubbed Zipper's mane.

"Fun?" Kendra groaned, spraying warm water over Star, her Welsh pony. "This is an awful job!"

"Cleaning your messy room would be an awful job," Ruth-Ann said. "But cleaning Star should be fun."

"That's easy for you to say," Kendra

replied. "You aren't trying to clean a snow-white pony."

"It's tough getting stains off a white horse," Megan agreed. "But Blondie is a Palomino, and they also look dirty easily. And even Zipper has a lot of white patches." Megan had finished washing Blondie, her half-Morgan Palomino pony, before the other girls had arrived. Now Blondie stood outside, quietly drying in the sunshine, while Megan helped Ruth-Ann bathe Zipper at the indoor wash rack.

Megan had promised to help her two friends. "I'll start with Zipper. He's as dirty as a pig! He's dirtier than a whole herd of pigs!"

"Bathing horses might be hard work," Ruth-Ann said, "but it's going to be worth it. Just think how incredible our ponies are going to look tomorrow for the Fun Fair!"

"I'm afraid I won't be able to go to the Fun Fair," Kendra said.

"Why won't you be able to go?"

"Dead people can't go to Fun Fairs," Kendra moaned.

"You don't look dead to me!" Megan laughed.

"Not yet," Kendra said. "But I'm going to drown while cleaning this pony!" Kendra raised her hand and wiped water droplets off her face. She was soaking wet from the top of her brown hair to the bottom of her soggy blue jeans. Beside her stood Star, who was also dripping water from the tip of her perfect white ears all the way down to her small black hooves.

"Who's having the shower over there?" Ruth-Ann asked. "You or Star?"

"Shower?" Kendra snorted. "I'll show you a shower!" She raised the hose and sprayed a stream of warm water toward Ruth-Ann. Ruth-Ann ducked behind Zipper with a grin and continued to scrub.

Zipper should have been the easiest horse to keep clean. He was a sorrel, with reddish-brown hair the color of a shiny new penny.

But because he was a Paint, he also had a lot of large white patches.

Ruth-Ann loved imagining what Zipper's patches might look like. The side nearest her had a strange spot that she thought looked a bit like an angry lobster with an open claw. His left ribcage had an even larger spot that looked something like a lopsided baby reaching his hands upward. Two of Zipper's legs were white from his body down to his hoof. All those patches were difficult to clean.

"Zipper's legs are hard to keep white, but his face is the worst!" Ruth-Ann said, adding more shampoo to her bucket of water. "Horses with bald faces are really awful to clean, especially if the skin on their nose is pink, like Zipper's." (A horse with a bald face doesn't have a hairless face. Either they have a very wide blaze that extends past their eyes or a totally white head.) In Zipper's case, his head was all white except for two big brown patches that surrounded his eyes, making it appear he was wearing glasses.

"I think Zipper really believes he is a pig," Megan agreed. "And we all know that pigs like to wallow with their little pink snouts in the mud."

"Well, I'm just about finished cleaning Zipper's snout," Ruth-Ann said. "And next I have to clean behind his ears." She stood on tiptoes to reach the top of Zipper's head and scrubbed gently. Zipper sighed and kept his head low so the girls could finish their work.

"Be careful you don't get that soapy water in Zipper's eyes," Megan warned. "The shampoo bottle says it won't sting, but I don't think we should find out."

"I'll be careful," Ruth-Ann said. "And Zipper's being such a good boy. I'm sure he's never been bathed before, but he's acting like an angel!"

"First you say he's a pig, and now you say he's an angel," Kendra said. "Can't you two make up your minds?"

"And if Zipper is acting like an angel, does that mean he's holding a harp and flying around?" Megan teased.

"My mom says real angels are busy," Kendra said. "They don't spend all their time flying around playing the harp. Instead they work for God. And they try to help people."

"Well, Zipper isn't busy," Ruth-Ann said. "In fact, I think he's almost asleep."

"He's a sleeping angel," Kendra said.

"He's a sleeping piglet," Megan replied.

Zipper yawned and closed his eyes halfway. But if Ruth-Ann had looked a little closer, she would have seen Zipper's eyes were twinkling mischievously behind his long brown lashes.

The girls continued to talk, and Zipper rested quietly. But when Ruth-Ann bent over to rinse her sponge, Zipper saw his opportunity. He opened his eyes slowly and looked around the wash rack. His bright brown eyes took in everything around him. He slowly raised one front hoof, and then with a surprisingly quick movement he pawed forward. He managed to reach the water bucket, which was half filled with soapy water. In an instant, water sprayed everywhere. Ruth-Ann let out a shriek as the water splashed across her clothing and filled her rubber boots.

Zipper seemed pleased with himself. He gave a horsy grin and then shook like a wet dog. The shower of water droplets finished soaking Ruth-Ann and Megan.

Everyone laughed. Zipper bobbed his head and shook again. *Bathing is a lot of fun!* Zipper seemed to say. *Especially if we all bathe together!*

"Oh, Ruth-Ann!" Kendra called cheerfully. "Now who's having a shower? You or Zipper?"

"Ha! Ha!" Ruth-Ann said. She wiped dirty bubbles off her cheek and shook water out of her short blackish-brown hair.

"Maybe Zipper isn't an angel after all," Megan said.

"He is, too," Ruth-Ann said. "He was being a helpful angel."

"Helpful?" Megan asked. "How was dumping water on us helpful?"

"Zipper knew Kendra was feeling discouraged," Ruth-Ann said. "And he wanted to cheer her up!"

"It worked!" Kendra said, laughing. "I feel much better now that everyone's soaking wet like me!"

Hoof
Black

Ruth-Ann wrung water out of her shirt sleeves and turned back to finish scrubbing Zipper's face. It was important that the ponies look their best for the Sedgewick Adventist Church Fun Fair the next day. The church was raising money for children who live at a Mexican orphanage. There would be booths with games such as dart throwing and ball toss. Ruth-Ann's mother was running a Fishing Pond, where the younger children could fish for small toys. Other adults would be selling slices of pizza and ice-cream floats.

Kendra's father had rented a cotton candy machine. "It looks simple," he had said, after reading the instructions that came with the machine. "All I need is white sugar and flavoring. And food coloring, of course. But what color of cotton candy should I make? The traditional pink or blue? Or maybe something totally different, like green or yellow? Hmmm . . . this could be fun!"

The Ready to Ride Club had found their decision of what to do simpler than reading Mr. Rawling's instruction book. "We can give pony rides!" they shouted together.

They had decided to wash the ponies at Megan's place the day before the fair. Mrs. Lewis had a wonderful indoor wash rack, with warm running water and rubber mats for the ponies to stand on. Ruth-Ann had collected bags of various colored ribbons from her mom's craft drawer so that they could braid Zipper's, Star's, and Blondie's manes. Kendra had bought a container of black hoof polish with money she'd saved from her tenth birthday. "We want the ponies to look special," Kendra had said.

18

When the girls were finally finished with the baths, they stepped back and admired their work. "We can't put hoof black on Star and Zipper's hooves until they're totally dry," Kendra said. "But we could all work together on Blondie."

Megan had shown horses with her mother and older sister, so she had learned how to apply hoof black. She carefully painted Blondie's hooves with the new hoof polish while the other girls found the big bag packed full of colored ribbons.

Kendra stood behind Blondie and began to braid her long, creamy tail. At the top of the braid she attached a bright green ribbon. Ruth-Ann worked on Blondie's mane, putting in dozens of small braids and fastening the ends with more green bows. When Megan was finished with Blondie's hooves, she straightened up. "Green looks perfect in Blondie's creamy mane," she said with a contented sigh.

When they were finished with Blondie

they moved over to Star, who was now dry. "I'll have to be extra careful with the hoof polish," Megan said as she bent over by the Welsh pony's feet. "Black polish would look awful if I accidentally get it on Star's white legs!" She slowly dabbed the polish on each hoof while the other girls braided blue ribbons into Star's long, flowing mane and tail.

"OK, Zipper," Ruth-Ann said when Star was totally braided and polished. "Now it's your turn."

"Zipper's a gelding," Kendra said. "Is it OK if boy horses wear hoof polish?"

Megan nodded her head. "My mom's big Morgan is a gelding, and his hooves are always polished for shows. Mom says it makes his legs look long and elegant."

"Could I try polishing Zipper's feet?" Ruth-Ann asked, picking up the small container. "I'll be really careful."

"You're an artist," Megan said. "So you'll probably do a neater job than I do! But you don't want to spill any polish on yourself.

It doesn't come off very easily, even with soapy water."

"I'll go slow," Ruth-Ann said. "And I'm wearing work clothes. Mom knew I'd get dirty." She unscrewed the lid and dipped the foam brush into the pot of black hoof coloring. Then she bent in front of Zipper and began to paint his right front hoof. She started at the middle of the hoof and worked upwards, being especially cautious when she was near the cornet band, where Zipper's black hoof and brown leg joined.

"That's perfect," Megan said. "You'd better watch out, or my mother will hire you to help her get horses ready to show!"

"That would be fun!" Ruth-Ann said. "Maybe I'll even learn how to show horses myself."

"That's what the Ready to Ride Club should do!" Kendra said. "We should have our own little horse show."

"We could have Western classes," Megan said.

"And English too," Kendra replied. "And maybe even some jumping."

"I want to learn to jump too," Ruth-Ann said. "But I don't know if Zipper would be a good jumper. He's pretty lazy."

"Zipper could learn how to jump," Megan said. "If he wanted to."

Ruth-Ann finished with Zipper's first hoof and moved to the right back leg. This hoof was even more tricky to polish since that leg was white right down to the hoof. "Don't wiggle, Zipper," Ruth-Ann breathed, moving the brush slowly. She was afraid that a fly or mosquito would bother Zipper and he would stomp a foot, but the horse stayed quite still while she worked underneath him. The other two girls began to braid his mane and tail with small red ribbons.

"Red looks nice on Zipper," Kendra said.

"And it will match his new saddle blanket," Ruth-Ann agreed. She moved around the horse and bent over to paint his left front hoof.

"We really shouldn't put a red bow in Zipper's tail," Megan said, adjusting the ribbon that she had fastened in the horse's sorrel tail.

"Why not?"

"People put red bows on their horse's tails to warn that they kick," Megan said. "And we know that Zipper would never kick anyone."

"Zipper never kicks," Ruth-Ann agreed. "A few months ago my little sister ran behind him and hugged his back legs, and he didn't move an inch!"

"What did you do?" Kendra asked.

"I didn't do anything," Ruth-Ann said. "But my mom sure did!" Ruth-Ann set the small jar of hoof polish down on the ground and dipped the sponge into the black paint.

Zipper peered down at the girl kneeling beside him. Then he looked at the jar of hoof polish. He seemed to remember just how much fun it had been to knock over the bucket of water.

Zipper studied the other girls. They were all too busy to notice the expression of concentration on his face. Zipper slowly raised his right front hoof and with a firm tap he bumped the container.

Black hoof dye splattered everywhere!

It splashed across the rubber mats and onto the nearby barn walls. Several huge drops sprayed across Ruth-Ann's rubber boots. And an enormous streak of black splattered across both of Zipper's front legs!

"Zipper!" Ruth-Ann screamed and whirled around to find the soapy wash cloth. She scrubbed frantically at the black dye on the little horse's legs.

The black color didn't wash off. Instead it smeared and spread upward. Ruth-Ann scrubbed even harder, and the spots grew bigger, and then bigger again.

"Stop!" Megan said. "It isn't going to come off."

"I need more soap!"

"Believe me, soap won't help," Megan said. "Nothing washes off hoof polish."

Ruth-Ann stopped rubbing. She looked at Zipper and then back at her friends. "What am I going to do?"

"You can't do anything," Megan said. "Hoof black lasts for days, but it will slowly wear off. Until then he'll have black legs."

"But Zipper looks awful!"

"Maybe he'll look like a bay instead of a sorrel," Kendra said. "Bay horses have black legs." The corners of Kendra's mouth twitched, but she didn't smile.

"Are you trying to be funny?" Ruth-Ann asked.

Megan bit her lip. "Maybe the red ribbon in Zipper's tail does suit him after all," she said slowly.

"How?"

Megan and Kendra looked at each other and then back at Zipper. "A red ribbon is supposed to be for a kicker," Megan said, beginning to giggle. "And now we've seen that Zipper does kick after all!"

The girls burst into laughter. Ruth-Ann laughed so hard she had to lean against the barn wall to catch her breath. When they were finally finished, Kendra had another thought.

"Zipper kicks," she said. "But he kicks with his front feet."

Ruth-Ann grinned at her R2R friends. "Zipper wasn't kicking," she said. "He just thought that since he was a Paint horse, he should actually paint himself! And the only color he had was black!"

Checking Out
the Fun Fair

"There are my parents," Megan said, waving her hand. The three girls had arrived at the Fun Fair almost an hour early so they would have time to prepare for the pony rides.

Mr. and Mrs. Lewis did not regularly attend church, but they had wanted to help earn money for the Mexican orphanage. The day before, they had created a large rope ring where the girls would do their pony rides. Now Mr. Lewis was hammering a wooden sign into the ground that said in big letters, "**PONY RIDES $1.00**."

"You girls look wonderful in your fancy riding clothes," Mrs. Lewis said admiringly.

She scratched Blondie's shoulder with a smile. "And your ponies are so clean."

The girls had dressed in outfits that matched their pony's ribbons. Ruth-Ann was wearing a new red Western shirt, and Zipper wore a scarlet saddle pad. Kendra was riding English, wearing a black jacket and bright blue shirt to match the bows in Star's mane and tail. Megan had borrowed a dark green Western shirt from her sister's closet that coordinated perfectly with Blondie's green ribbons.

Their riding instructor, Trish Klein, strolled over. "Hi girls," she said. "How are your ponies behaving today?"

"They're good," Ruth-Ann said, dismounting from the Paint horse. "Except Zipper slept in the dirt again last night."

"We had to quickly wash the left side of his head this morning," Megan said. "And all his white spots on the left side of his body, too."

"And he rubbed out a whole bunch of his braids," Ruth-Ann reported. "So we had to quickly redo them."

"We had to replace some of Star's braids too," Kendra said.

"We think Zipper pulled them out," Megan said. "With his teeth."

"He even had a piece of red ribbon stuck between his front teeth!" Ruth-Ann snorted.

"Well, you did an excellent job repairing everything," Trish said. "Because they all look quite lovely now."

"Except for the hoof polish all across Zipper's front legs," Ruth-Ann said. "I hope no one thinks it's mud." She rubbed on the now dry black spots and sighed.

"No one will notice a thing," Trish reassured them. "And how they look isn't as important as how they behave. Today you'll have lots of young and inexperienced riders wanting pony rides, and it's important that we keep everyone safe."

"We brought our helmets," Ruth-Ann said. She reached up and knocked on her bright-pink helmet. "I know it doesn't match my saddle blanket, but Mom wouldn't let me ride without it. And I brought my little sister's helmet, too, in case we have some really small riders."

Mrs. Lewis held up two larger helmets that belonged to the Lewis family. "So we'll have six different helmets," she said. "We should be able to fit almost any size head."

"Helmets are an important part of safety," Trish said. "But they're only one part. I'm hoping that Mr. and Mrs. Lewis will walk beside the smallest riders to assist their balance while you girls lead the ponies. I will stay at the gate and keep an eye on everyone. If I see anything that could startle the ponies or hurt a rider, I want to be able to step in quickly to help."

"I'm a bit nervous," Megan said slowly. "Blondie hasn't been ridden by little kids before. What will I do if she starts behaving badly?"

"Blondie will be fine," Mrs. Lewis said. "She's seen a lot of children at our horse shows."

"But they weren't riding her," Megan said. "What if a little kid accidentally kicks her too hard or does something to scare her?"

"That's why your parents and I are here," Trish said. "We will keep an eye on the ponies. If they start looking frightened or angry or even overtired, then we will stop the ride. It's important that we keep everyone safe."

"I'm pretty certain Zipper will be relaxed," Ruth-Ann said. "Mikey and Lisa ride him every day. He's used to noisy, wiggly children."

"I think Star will be OK too," Kendra said.

"I expect all your horses will be well behaved," Trish said. "But don't forget, sometimes strange things can happen. I've seen calm, well-trained horses frightened by unexpected things such as sirens and firecrackers and flags blowing in the wind."

"You're making me more nervous!" Megan said.

"I have one last suggestion that might make you feel a bit better," Trish said. "I think it would be a good idea for us to pray right now, before the rides start."

"We're going to pray that I'm not so nervous?" Megan asked.

Trish smiled. "Yes," she said. "We'll pray that you won't feel so nervous. But we also should pray that God keeps everyone safe. God is better protection than any helmet!"

"That's a great idea," Kendra said.

"Wait," Kendra said. "I'll dismount before we pray. It would be good if Star had a rest before the pony rides." Kendra and Megan dismounted and stood by their ponies while Trish bent her head. Even Mr. and Mrs. Lewis bowed their heads and closed their eyes.

"Dear Lord," Trish prayed. "You know that we want to help earn money for the children in Mexico today. Please help the Fun Fair to go well and earn a lot of money for this cause. Please be with all the people here, and watch over them and keep them safe. We ask for a special blessing on Megan, Kendra, and Ruth-Ann and their ponies now. Please keep us from being nervous, but help us to remember to still pay attention to any potential problems. We know that all sports can be dangerous sometimes, and we don't want anyone to get hurt today. Please help Star, Blondie, and Zipper be good, and be with the Lewis family, and me too. Amen."

Everyone opened their eyes. "Look," Ruth-Ann said, pointing at her horse. "Zipper has his eyes closed too. Maybe he was praying!"

"He's an angel," Kendra said. "Remember?" The three girls grinned, remembering the shower Zipper gave them all a day earlier.

"That was a nice prayer," Mrs. Lewis said. "I've never heard anyone pray for a horse before."

"Oh, I believe that God's interested in everything in our lives," Trish said. "And we know that He cares for the animals. The Bible says that God even watches over the sparrows."

Mrs. Lewis nodded thoughtfully.

The girls loosened their ponies' girths. "We'll let them relax for a while," Megan said. "Is there anything else we need to do, Mom?"

"I think we're totally ready," Mrs. Lewis replied. "Things won't start for about half an hour."

"I'll keep an eye on the ponies if you girls want to walk around and look at everything," Mr. Lewis offered. "You won't have time once the pony rides begin." The three girls tied the ponies to a nearby fence and then wandered around the big school grounds.

Mrs. Chow was putting some last-minute touches on her fishing pond booth. "Hi girls!" she called.

"Ruthie!" Ruth-Ann's two-year-old brother, Mikey, and four-year-old sister, Lisa, stopped arguing over a toy fishing pole for a minute to wave at the girls. The members of the Ready to Ride Club paused to admire the fishing pond and then moved on to see what else was happening.

Kendra's father was easy to find. The delicious smell of cotton candy filled the air, but Mr. Rawling appeared frazzled. "Black cotton candy!" he groaned as the girls approached. "Who wants to buy black cotton candy?"

"What's wrong, Dad?" Kendra asked.

"Nothing's wrong," Mr. Rawling said. "If you like to eat cotton candy that's the color of dirt."

"Dirt?"

"Or mud," the man said. He reached into his booth and brought out a bag of cotton candy.

It was a strange color. It wasn't black, exactly. But it certainly wasn't the normal blue or pink that the girls had come to expect from cotton candy at the fair. Instead it was a dirty blackish-gray tone.

"What happened?" Ruth-Ann asked.

"I wanted to make some unique cotton candy," Mr. Rawling said. "I thought I'd make purple, so I added some blue and pink coloring together."

"Purple's a nice color," Megan said.

"This isn't purple," Kendra said.

"I know!" Mr. Rawling said.

"Why isn't it purple?"

"I was in a rush," Mr. Rawling said, "And I accidentally put in too much blue. The color got too dark, so I thought I'd add a whole bunch of yellow coloring to make it lighter."

"Mr. Rawling!" Ruth-Ann said. "Haven't you taken art class?"

"You're the artist, Ruth-Ann," Mr. Rawling said. "Not me!'

"But—"

"I'm just a poor business man, struggling to make a living," Mr. Rawling continued with a groan. "I just try to put food on the table, and hay in Star's feed trough! I didn't know what would happen when I mixed all the colors together."

"All the colors?"

"I had to add some green," Mr. Rawling said. "I thought it would look better. And when that didn't help I added some more red."

"How does it taste?" Megan asked.

"It takes good," Mr. Rawling said. "But no one's going to try it!"

"Well, you wanted unique cotton candy, Dad," Kendra said. "And this is unique."

"I have an idea," Megan said. "Why don't you pretend you wanted it to be that color, and give it a fancy name? Kids love things that are different."

"A fancy name?" Mr. Rawling said. "What am I going to call it? Squished frog? Rotten banana? Mud puddle?"

"I'd stay away from the squished frog idea, Dad," Kendra said. "But mud puddle sounds OK. Boys love food with names like that."

"Sure they do," Ruth-Ann agreed. "And girls do too. Think of all the good things that have strange names. There's rocky road ice-cream—everyone loves that!"

"And I've heard of chocolate mud pie before," Megan said.

"My first-grade teacher made 'dirt' cupcakes with Oreo cookie crumbs on top to look like the ground, and little gummy worms sticking their heads out," Kendra said. "Everyone thought they were cute!"

"Gummy worms!" Ruth-Ann said. "If you put a gummy worm in each bag of cotton candy the kids would go crazy!"

"Is that a good thing?" Mr. Rawling asked.

"It is if you want to sell lots of cotton candy," Ruth-Ann said.

"Well, I don't know about dirt cotton candy and gummy worms," Mr. Rawling said. "But maybe there is a way I could turn my disaster into a success. At least you girls gave me an idea or two. How did you get to be so smart?"

"It's a girl thing," Kendra said, grinning at her father. "A Ready to Ride girl thing!"

"Actually," Ruth-Ann said, "I think it's a God thing more than a girl thing. Trish prayed that we'd all have a good day today. And I'm sure God doesn't want your cotton candy ruined, Mr. Rawling. The money's for the little kids in Mexico."

Mr. Rawling nodded, for once looking serious. "You girls *are* smart," he said. "And I'm really glad you're so smart about God. I've been so busy worrying about this cotton candy I honestly didn't take the time to pray. But I will now. With prayer, and your help, my strange-looking cotton candy might turn out fine after all."

As the girls walked back toward their ponies and the riding ring, they could hear Mr. Rawling talking out loud to himself. "What else is dark colored? Ebony? Tar? Coal? Night-time? Hmm."

Perfect
Pony Rides

By four o'clock in the afternoon a line of children and parents had formed at the Pony Ride sign. The girls quickly tightened their ponies' cinches and led them into the rope ring.

"I'm still a little nervous," Megan whispered to Ruth-Ann.

"Me too," Ruth-Ann whispered back.

But Ruth-Ann didn't have time to worry for long. Trish directed a trio of children into the ring for their pony rides. Zipper's first rider was a small girl with long blond hair. The girl bounced over to Zipper with a huge grin.

"Your horsy is really nice," she said, adjusting her riding helmet. "I picked him because he's the biggest. I like big horses."

Ruth-Ann smiled and held Zipper still while Mrs. Lewis lifted the girl onto the horse's back.

"I'm Crystal," the girl said. "Can your horse go fast?" She picked up the reins and gave them a shake. "Go horsy," she said.

"Zipper can go fast," Ruth-Ann said. "But we have to walk today."

"I want to go fast!"

"We have to follow the rules," Ruth-Ann said. "Otherwise someone could be hurt."

"I won't get hurt," the girl said. "I'm a good horse rider."

"Do you need help?" Mrs. Lewis asked. "I can walk beside you."

"I can ride alone," the girl said quickly. "I'm six years old, and I know a lot about horses." Mrs. Lewis looked over at the girl's mother, who nodded that it would be OK for her to ride without assistance.

Ruth-Ann clicked her tongue and led Zipper forward. They began to circle the small riding ring. "What sort of things do you know about horses?" Ruth-Ann asked.

"I know what type of horse this is," the little girl said. "I have a whole bunch of horse books, you know. And this horse is an Appaloosa."

"Zipper isn't an Appaloosa," Ruth-Ann said. "He's a Paint."

"Appaloosas have spots," the girl said. "And this horse has spots."

"Appaloosas have little spots," Ruth-Ann said. "Their spots can look like freckles. Zipper has great big spots, almost like patches of white."

"Oh," the little girl said. "Why do you call your horsy Zipper?"

"His registered name is Zippitty Do Dah," Ruth-Ann said. "But that would be too hard to say. So we call him Zipper for short." They circled the ring three times and then came to a halt.

"Time to hop off, Crystal," the mother said. But the blond-haired girl clutched the saddle horn.

"I want another turn," she said, her face beaming happily. "I like Zipper. And he likes me."

"You can have another turn," the mother agreed. "But we have to go to the back of the line now, and let someone else ride first."

"Maybe you'll want to ride a different pony next time," Mrs. Lewis said. She helped the girl dismount and unsnapped the riding helmet.

"I don't want to ride another pony," the girl said. She stood on tiptoes and hugged Zipper's neck. "This one's the best! My daddy gave me five dollars, and I'm going to spend it all riding Zipper!"

Ruth-Ann could hear the little girl chattering as she walked back into line for her next turn. "And he's a Paint," she told her mother. "Not an Appaloosa. Appaloosas have little spots, Mom, not big ones like Zipper."

One person after another rode the patient ponies around the ring. Many of the parents purposely waited for Star or Blondie because they wanted a smaller pony for their young children. Several bigger children rode Zipper, choosing him because of his larger size.

Ruth-Ann's little sister, Lisa, soon appeared for a pony ride. "I wanna ride Zipper," the four-year-old said.

"Why don't you ride Star or Blondie?" Mrs. Chow suggested. "You can ride Zipper at home anytime you want. For free."

"Zipper's the best," Lisa insisted. She held her dollar out to Trish, who took it with a smile.

Mrs. Chow shrugged her shoulders and helped boost the little girl onto Zipper's back. "We only have time for one ride," she said. "And then we have to get back to the Fishing Booth. Daddy's going to be very busy watching over both the booth and Mikey!"

All the ponies were behaving very well. Even Blondie appeared calm and relaxed as she circled the rope ring with various children on her back.

Before long the little blond-haired girl was back. She chattered loudly to Ruth-Ann as they walked around the ring. "And if Zipper was my pony I'd put purple ribbons in his mane," she said. "Purple's my favorite color. See? My shirt's purple. Then Zipper and I would match. We could be twins."

Ruth-Ann smiled and didn't say anything.

"I could buy a purple riding helmet," she said. "And purple cowboy boots. Do they make purple cowboy boots?"

"I don't know," Ruth-Ann said.

"I could paint my cowboy boots purple," the blond-haired girl said. "That would look nice. And . . ."

When they returned to starting line, Ruth-Ann found Mr. Rawling waiting for a ride.

"I didn't know you liked horses," Ruth-Ann said. She held Zipper still while Mr.

Rawling carefully poked his foot in the stirrup and struggled to mount.

"Like horses?" Mr. Rawling said. "I don't like horses. I hate them!"

"Then why are you here for a ride on Zipper?" Ruth-Ann asked.

"Star's too small for me," Mr. Rawling said. He grunted and finally got settled in the saddle. "If I rode Star she'd fall right over. I'd squish her as flat as a pancake. And that could be a problem! Who wants a big pony pancake? That would be harder to sell than black cotton candy!"

"You have a point there," Ruth-Ann agreed.

Mr. Rawling grabbed the saddle horn and nodded at Ruth-Ann. "Yee-haw!" he said. "Giddy up, hoss!" Ruth-Ann grinned and led Zipper forward.

"How *is* your cotton candy selling?" Ruth-Ann asked as they circled the ring. "Is anyone buying it?"

"I'm as busy as an octopus with nine legs!" Mr. Rawling said. "Everyone wants some of my world-famous midnight cotton candy!"

"Midnight cotton candy!" Ruth-Ann exclaimed. "You took our suggestion and gave it a fancy name!"

"I did," Mr. Rawling said. "And it was a good idea—considering that it was from a girl, that is! And the kids just love it. I sent Mrs. Rawling to the store for some fancy little candy stars. You know, the sugary decorations that can be used for icing on cakes? I put the stars into the dark cotton candy, and it looks like the night. Everyone loves it!"

"That's great."

"Fantastic," Mr. Rawling agreed. "Stupendous. First-rate. Terrific. And I owe it all to you girls. So thank you."

"You're welcome," Ruth-Ann said. They circled the ring three times and then halted. Mr. Rawling slid awkwardly off Zipper and gave the horse's neck a friendly pat before scratching Star and Blondie.

"I knew you liked horses," Kendra called to her father.

"I like them all right," Mr. Rawling said. "In soup and stew!"

"Daddy!" Kendra laughed. "You wouldn't eat a horse."

"How can you be certain?"

"You're a vegetarian!" Kendra said.

Mr. Rawling scratched his head. "I guess you got me there," he said. "Well, I better get back to the cotton candy stand. Who knows, maybe I've invented something new. I could make a million if I just patent my idea. Midnight cotton candy!"

Zipper and the Yellow Balloon

The Fun Fair was almost finished. Ruth-Ann's feet were sore from walking around and around the small ring in her riding boots. Zipper was still cheerful, but the bright red ribbon on his tail had long since fallen out and been trampled in the grass. The other ponies were also looking a bit bedraggled. Star even had a big patch of dark sticky cotton candy caught in her mane from a young rider who was trying to eat while riding.

"Pony rides will be finished in ten minutes," Mr. Lewis announced to the small group of people who still stood at the gate waiting for rides.

Megan's older sister, Mandy, stepped forward, pushing a large teenage boy in front of her. "Tyler needs to ride before the Fun Fair ends," she said.

"That's Tyler Anderson, my sister's new boyfriend," Megan hissed, "but I don't think he likes horses."

Mandy led the boy over to Ruth-Ann and Zipper. "Tyler's too big for the little ponies," Mandy announced. "So he'll ride Zipper."

"Do you actually want to ride, Tyler?" Mr. Lewis asked.

Tyler shrugged his shoulders. "I guess so," he said. "I paid that lady my last dollar."

"Put your foot in the stirrup and hop on," Mandy said. She twisted the stirrup for the boy, but he hesitated.

"Maybe I'm too big for this pony," Tyler said slowly.

"Zipper's not a pony," Ruth-Ann said. "He's a horse. And he can easily carry someone your size."

"Does he ever buck?"

"Don't be silly!" Mandy scoffed. "Of course he doesn't buck! Didn't you see all the little kids riding him around the ring? They didn't get bucked off."

"Mandy," Mrs. Lewis interrupted. "Please don't make Tyler ride if he doesn't want to. Not everyone likes horse riding."

"I like horse riding," Tyler said. "I think."

He took a step closer to Zipper and looked up at the saddle. "You need to put your foot in the stirrup," Ruth-Ann said. "I won't be able to lift you."

Tyler hesitantly lifted his leg and put his toe in the stirrup. With a grunt he managed to get up into the saddle.

Ruth-Ann had to bite her lip so she didn't laugh. The boy's long legs were bent almost in two to fit in the short kid's stirrups. Tyler didn't seem to find anything funny. He sheepishly reached forward and grabbed hold of the saddle horn with both hands.

Ruth-Ann clicked her tongue and walked Zipper forward.

"Are those the brakes?" Tyler asked after they circled the ring once. He looked down at the reins that dangled on Zipper's neck.

"We're just going to walk," Ruth-Ann said. "And I can stop Zipper with the lead rope. If you were riding alone, you'd need to use the reins to turn and stop him."

"Like this?" Tyler asked. He freed one hand from the saddle horn and grabbed hold of the reins. When Zipper felt the boy pull, he came to a halt.

"That's right," Ruth-Ann said. "But pull softer. And once Zipper stops you need to let the reins loose again. That's his reward for obeying you."

Tyler moved his hands forward, and Zipper started back into a walk.

"That's neat," Tyler said. "Can I do it again?"

Ruth-Ann nodded. Tyler pulled back awkwardly on the reins, and again Zipper came to a stop.

"Have you ever ridden a horse before?" Ruth-Ann asked.

Tyler shook his head. "Mandy wants me to learn to ride horses," he said. "I think she rides all the time."

"You're doing a really good job," Ruth-Ann said.

Tyler looked around him and seemed to relax a little. "Yeah," he said. "I guess I'm doing OK. At least I haven't fallen off yet!" He moved his hand forward, and the pair started to circle the ring again. In a few moments the boy took his other hand off the saddle horn to wave at Mandy.

"How do people learn to ride horses?" Tyler asked.

"The same way you learn anything," Ruth-Ann said. "You take lessons from a good teacher, and then you practice a lot."

"I wouldn't want to take lessons from Mandy," Tyler said. "She'd be too bossy!"

"Trish is a good trainer," Ruth-Ann said, pointing at the woman who stood at the gate of the riding ring. "She could teach you how to ride."

"Maybe I could take some lessons," Tyler said. "How much do they cost? This hasn't been as tough as I'd thought it would be."

Suddenly Ruth-Ann caught a glimpse of something bright yellow out of the corner of her eye. It was a helium balloon. A child had just dropped the string of the balloon, and it blew in a sudden gust of wind straight toward Zipper.

Before Ruth-Ann could do anything, the balloon careened forward and struck Zipper on the side of the head!

Zipper didn't have time to think. Instead he jumped forward with his eyes as wide as dinner plates. The balloon slid along Zipper's right side and then shot over his back and into the air.

As soon as the balloon was gone, Zipper came to an immediate halt. Tyler wasn't prepared for the sudden start and stop. He bobbed backward with Zipper's first jump, and when the horse stopped he lurched ahead and fell onto Zipper's neck.

One hand grabbed for Zipper's mane, but it was too late. Tyler slid sideways out of the saddle and toppled off Zipper. He hit the grass with a thud.

Zipper looked puzzled. He lowered his head and sniffed the boy's back. *What are you doing down there?* he seemed to wonder.

The other ponies came to a halt.

Mr. and Mrs. Lewis rushed over, with Mandy and Trish on their heels. They helped Tyler to his feet. "Are you OK?" Mrs. Lewis asked.

"Let me check your arm," Mr. Lewis said.

"Did you bump your head?" Trish asked.

Tyler looked at the grass marks on his pants. He looked at the bit of dirt that was stuck to his hands, and then he looked over at Zipper, who was now standing calmly with an expression on his face that seemed to say *Oh, it was just a balloon. My mistake.*

"That's a crazy horse," the boy said sharply. "He could have killed me."

"I'm so sorry," Ruth-Ann began, but she didn't have a chance to say anything else before Tyler interrupted her.

"I've never seen such a horrible horse!" he said in a louder voice. "He's vicious. That's what he is. You shouldn't have an animal at a place like this. Someone could be seriously hurt."

"The balloon in the wind—" Mrs. Lewis said.

"I could have been killed!" Tyler said. "Did you see the way he bucked? That's a dangerous horse." He wiped the dirt off his hands and then spun around and stomped off.

"Zipper didn't buck," Ruth-Ann said. "And he isn't dangerous. He was just frightened of the balloon."

Tyler stalked out of the ring. At the gate he pulled off his riding helmet and tossed it behind him into the long grass. Then he was gone, with Mandy trailing behind him.

Ruth-Ann looked around at the crowd. They were all staring at her and Zipper. She felt her face begin to turn red. How embarrassing!

"Pony rides are over," Mr. Lewis announced. "The Fair closes in a few minutes, anyhow. We want to thank you all for having rides with us."

The crowd slowly began to drift away.

"That was interesting," Kendra said slowly. "I guess."

"I didn't think Zipper was ever scared of anything," Ruth-Ann said.

"Zipper's a horse," Trish said. She came over and stroked the Paint's neck. "Don't forget, all horses are prey animals. Some are braver than others, but they all survive in the wild by escaping dangerous situations. That balloon startled Zipper, and he jumped without thinking."

"It's a good thing Tyler wasn't riding Blondie," Megan said. "She was frightened by the balloon, and it didn't even come close to her!"

"I should have been more prepared," Ruth-Ann said. She suddenly felt her eyes prick with tears of embarrassment. "Maybe I could have stopped Zipper from jumping forward."

"No," Trish said. "I think we were very well prepared. We did everything possible to prevent anyone from being hurt. We had an enclosed ring, and lots of helpers, and everyone rode with a helmet. But sometimes things just happen."

"But why do they have to happen to us?" Ruth-Ann asked, trying to smile.

"When people learn to ride bikes, they fall and sometimes get hurt," Trish said. "And when people learn to skateboard or snowboard or ski, they also fall sometimes. All sports have risks. We just need to keep the risks as low as possible."

"Tyler was so mad at us," Megan said.

"He was mad at *me!*" Ruth-Ann said. "And Zipper."

"Tyler was scared," Trish said. "Sometimes people become angry when they're afraid. Maybe we can call him later tonight and see how he's doing when things calm down."

"I don't want to call him," Ruth-Ann said.

"I will," Trish promised. "And I'll pray that God gives me the right words to encourage Tyler. I wouldn't want him to be afraid of all horses because of a one-time event."

"Why didn't God keep Tyler safe?" Megan asked. Ruth-Ann noticed that Megan's parents were listening in the background for Trish's answer.

"God did keep Tyler safe," Trish said. "He could have been seriously hurt, and instead he just bumped his knees."

"But why did he even have to fall off?"

"Girls," Trish said with a sigh. "It would be a lie if I said I always understand how God works. I do know that He cares for each of us. He knows how many hairs we

59

have on our head. But I also know there are a lot of bad things in this world. Sometimes we can see the reason why things happen, and sometimes we'll never know until we get to heaven."

The girls were quiet as they rode their ponies home that afternoon. Ruth-Ann wasn't certain if she should be happy about the day, or not.

The Pony Rides had earned more than fifty-five dollars for the Mexican orphanage. The ponies had all been very good except for the incident with Zipper and the yellow balloon. Many children had loved their pony rides.

But Tyler wasn't one of them.

Zipper Staples Himself

Mr. Chow was not happy. "Chickens are the dumbest birds alive," he muttered. He pulled the wire mesh tight and stapled it to the chicken coop. "And if they aren't careful, they're going to be the dumbest birds *dead,* too. Sometimes I think chickens just want something to eat them."

"What's wrong, Dad?" Ruth-Ann asked. She glanced at Zipper, who stood nearby with his head hanging over the corral fence. Ruth-Ann hoped Zipper wasn't causing problems with the chickens. The previous year the little Paint had learned how to use his teeth to open the gate to the chicken run. Mr. Chow had finally put a horse-proof snap on the gate. But now Ruth-Ann wondered if Zipper had found another way to set the chickens free.

"It isn't Zipper's fault this time," Mr. Chow said, guessing Ruth-Ann's thoughts. "The chickens are escaping on their own."

"How?"

"They've discovered they can squeeze between the wire and the boards," Mr. Chow said. "Last night half the flock was loose."

"I know what happened," Ruth-Ann said with a grin. "The smart chickens found a way out, and the stupid ones were left behind!"

"There's no such thing as a smart chicken," Mr. Chow replied. He hammered another staple into the board that ran along the bottom of the chicken run, and stood back to look. "There," he muttered. "That should hold them for a few more days."

An ear-piercing shriek came from the Chow house. Mr. Chow raised his eyebrows and turned to Ruth-Ann. "Mikey?" he asked.

"I wonder what he's up to now?" Ruth-Ann asked.

There was another loud bellow. Mr. Chow sighed and put down his bucket of staples. "Hopefully we don't have to visit the doctor again this week," he said.

On the previous Monday, two-year-old Mikey had stuck a dried lima bean up his nose, forcing a trip to the local doctor's office. And a few weeks earlier he had fallen off his tricycle and needed three stitches to the back of his head. So Ruth-Ann and her father had a reason to worry.

This time the problem wasn't so serious and didn't involve either dried beans or stitches. Mrs. Chow had set the table for supper and then walked downstairs for a jar of canned fruit. When Mikey was certain his mother was out of sight, he'd pulled on the long tablecloth to try to reach a glass of juice. Several dishes had tumbled off the table, and a big serving spoon had struck Mikey right in the middle of his forehead.

"I wan' more juice," Mikey cried as they came into the house.

"He's lucky something else didn't hit him," Mrs. Chow said as she picked up pieces of broken dish from the kitchen floor.

Mr. Chow snorted.

When supper was finished, Ruth-Ann helped clear the table and then headed back outside. She planned to take Zipper for a short ride, but when she got close to the corral, she saw the little Paint horse had made a terrible mess.

Zipper had somehow stretched his neck far enough to pick up the pail of staples with his teeth. To his disappointment, the pail wasn't full of yummy grain, and he had eventually dropped it. Staples, hammer, and pliers lay covered in dirt on Zipper's side of the corral.

Ruth-Ann groaned and crawled under the fence. "You're as bad as Mikey," she said. "Trying to find something good to eat, and instead making a big mess. I just hope you weren't dumb enough to eat any staples! Or stick them up your nose!" She dug around in the dust, picking up everything within reach. Zipper stood over her, trying to be helpful by nuzzling her back every time she bent over. *There's another one over there,* he seemed to say.

When the mess was finally cleaned up, Ruth-Ann slipped on Zipper's halter and led him over to a nearby fence. "You're such a slow poke," she muttered as the horse dawdled behind her. "Exercise will be good for you."

She tied Zipper to a fence post and brought over a brush and hoof pick. Ruth-Ann carefully brushed the horse's back and sides, and then picked out his hooves.

When Ruth-Ann got to Zipper's left front foot she stopped. Something shiny glistened from Zipper's frog (the V-shaped cleft at the bottom of the hoof). Was it a piece of tinfoil or garbage from the Fun

Fair? She poked the hoof pick at the silver object.

Clink. The shiny object was hard. Ruth-Ann peered closer.

A metal fencing staple was stuck in Zipper's hoof!

Ruth-Ann tried to wedge the hoof pick under the staple, but it wouldn't fit. Zipper didn't seem that uncomfortable, and only flinched once when she tried to force the pick's point under the metal.

What should I do? Ruth-Ann asked herself, carefully setting Zipper's hoof down. She needed help. But her parents didn't have much experience with horses. The Lewises lived nearby. Perhaps Megan's mom would know how to help Zipper.

With one last glance at Zipper, Ruth-Ann darted into the house to phone.

Before long Mrs. Lewis and Megan arrived at the corral. Ruth-Ann's father also came outside, and he held Zipper's lead rope with a worried expression on his face.

"He wasn't limping," Ruth-Ann said. "So maybe it isn't too serious. But I didn't know what to do."

"It isn't bleeding," Mr. Chow said.

Mrs. Lewis sighed. "Puncture wounds in a horse's hoof are often more serious than they first appear," she said. She picked up the fencing pliers and used them to grab the top of the staple. It took her a few moments to get a firm grip on the staple, and Zipper fidgeted a bit, but before long she was able to yank the staple out of Zipper's hoof.

"Was it in really deep?" Ruth-Ann asked. She didn't want to look.

"There's only a tiny drop of blood," Mr. Chow said.

"I can't see a hole where the staple was," Megan said. "So maybe it's not so bad after all."

"Puncture wounds can get infected and abscess," Mrs. Lewis said. "A horse can be lame for months."

"We can't let that happen," Mr. Chow said. "Is there anything we can do?"

"I think we should phone the vet," Mrs. Lewis said. "Dr. Bob would probably want to put Zipper on some antibiotics to prevent an infection from starting."

Mr. Chow pulled out his cell phone and dialed a number. He spoke to the veterinarian's receptionist and then passed the phone to Mrs. Lewis. She spoke for several minutes to the vet and then hung up. "Dr. Bob suggests you put Zipper on antibiotics for a week. If you want, I can drive you over to the clinic and pick up the medication. And I'll help you with the first doses."

"Poor old Zipper," Mr. Chow said, stroking the horse's brown and white neck. "I always said you are a birdbrain. And now you proved it—taking dangerous chances just like the chickens!"

"I hope Zipper's medicine doesn't taste as bad as the stuff I had to take for my last ear infection," Ruth-Ann said.

"Don't you take pills?" Megan asked.

"I just can't swallow pills," Ruth-Ann

said. "So I have to take that gross liquid stuff."

"Ruth-Ann," Mrs. Lewis said. "Horses don't willingly swallow pills or take liquid medicine off a spoon like people do. Instead they normally get needles. I suspect Zipper will end up having a shot every day this week!"

Zipper's
Bad Medicine

In less than an hour the group was back by the corral. Ruth-Ann haltered Zipper again and led him to the wooden fence.

"Should I tie Zipper to the post?" she asked.

Mrs. Lewis shook her head. "No," she said. "Zipper might jump when I give him the injections, and I don't want him to pull back when he's tied."

"Injections?" Ruth-Ann asked. "Does he need more than one?"

"Dr. Bob says we have to give him three different injections." Mrs. Lewis sighed.

"Three injections!" Mr. Chow said. "Why three?"

"Horses are really big, and they need a lot of medicine," Mrs. Lewis said. "Dr. Bob told me that Zipper can only absorb so much medicine at one place. We have to divide it into three doses and poke him three times."

"Three times?" Ruth-Ann asked.

"Each day?" Mr. Chow asked.

"Three times, each day, for an entire week," Mrs. Lewis said. Ruth-Ann felt sick just thinking about it. But Zipper appeared quite unconcerned as Mrs. Lewis positioned him near the fence with Mr. Chow firmly holding the lead rope.

Mrs. Lewis stroked the horse's neck. "I'll poke him here," she said. "In the muscle on his neck." She took the plastic cap off the end of the syringe and with a quick motion poked Zipper.

Zipper jumped forward as though stung by a bee. Mrs. Lewis managed to push the plunger and get Zipper's medicine into him while Mr. Chow pulled on the lead rope and turned Zipper in a small circle.

"That's once," Mrs. Lewis said. "But I suspect the next two shots will be worse. Now Zipper knows what to expect."

They turned the little Paint so they could work on the opposite side of his neck. "Keep him close to the fence," Mrs. Lewis said. "That way he can't move sideways." She re-filled her syringe with medicine and then began to pat's Zipper's neck.

Zipper flinched and tried to back up. Mrs. Lewis followed him while Mr. Chow applied pressure to the lead rope. Before Mrs. Lewis could poke Zipper, he abruptly walked forward, now dragging Mr. Chow behind him.

"He knows it's coming," Mr. Chow said.

"I'll try to be quick," Mrs. Lewis said. She helped the man bring Zipper back up against the fence, and then rapidly jabbed her hand forward, poking Zipper's neck with the needle again.

This time Zipper jumped higher and far-ther forward, almost pulling Mr. Chow off his feet. Mrs. Lewis had to let go of the syringe, and as Ruth-Ann watched it wiggled in Zipper's neck like a dart in a dart-board. When Zipper finally paused Mrs. Lewis swiftly stepped forward and squeezed the syringe, injecting the medicine.

"That's two times," Megan said.

"Can't you poke him softer?" Ruth-Ann asked. Zipper turned his head and looked at her with an expression that seemed to say *Why aren't you helping me? I thought you were my friend!*

"I'm not a doctor," Mrs. Lewis said. "But I do know that a needle is much less painful if it goes through the skin quickly."

Zipper would not stand still for the third shot. Instead he wiggled and jerked and trotted around Mr. Chow. Zipper's head was high and his ears were back. The look in his eye was very wary whenever Mrs. Lewis moved in his direction. He stood for a moment and then pushed forward again, circling the pair at a choppy trot, and then stopped again.

Megan and Ruth-Ann both had to back out of the horse's way. "Doesn't Zipper know we're just trying to help him?" Megan asked.

"A horse is like a little kid," Mrs. Lewis said grimly. "They can't understand what you're doing. And while some children are quiet and cooperative for shots, many others cry and struggle and fight."

Ruth-Ann shuddered when she thought about how Mikey had acted because of the stitches in his head. It had taken two nurses to hold the little boy still while the doctor worked! And Zipper was much, much bigger than Mikey.

This time Mrs. Lewis was ready. When Zipper paused in his circle, she popped her hand forward and plunged the needle into his neck.

Zipper reared straight into the air! His front legs came forward, and he pawed at Mrs. Lewis. She jumped backward just in time, barely avoiding Zipper's sharp hooves.

"Bad horse!" Mr. Chow shouted. He jerked on the lead rope.

Mrs. Lewis was ready. As soon as Zipper's feet hit the ground, she darted forward and pushed the plunger of the syringe.

Zipper snorted and spun around. His ears were flat back against his head, and he rolled his eyes. *I hate you!* Zipper seemed to say. *Keep away from me, and don't hurt me anymore!*

Ruth-Ann was almost in tears as she led the horse back into his corral. She tossed a flake of sweet-smelling hay over the fence, but Zipper stood in the center and refused to come near. He didn't trust anyone for the moment.

Ruth-Ann stayed at the corral while everyone else left. Finally Zipper drifted over and began to eat. Every so often he raised his head and looked at Ruth-Ann. The expression in Zipper's eyes made Ruth-Ann feel terrible. It was as though Zipper blamed her for the shots! He didn't know why they had hurt him, and he was sad and mad and afraid all at the same time.

And Ruth-Ann felt exactly the same.

A Ready to Ride Meeting

"I don't know what to do," Ruth-Ann said. "Zipper's supposed to get three more needles again tomorrow! But Zipper's going to hate us all, and someone might get hurt!" Megan and Ruth-Ann explained everything to Kendra—how Zipper had struggled and fought and even struck out at Mrs. Lewis when she gave him the last shot.

The Ready to Ride Club had solved problems before, and they quickly passed around sheets of paper. "Write down why Zipper acted like that, and what we can do to help him," Megan said. She began to scribble on the paper.

Soon it was time for everyone to read out loud. Since Zipper was Ruth-Ann's horse, she went first.

"Zipper is very, very afraid. He's acting just like Mikey did when he got his stitches. Zipper doesn't know that the needles are supposed to help him. Instead he thinks we're attacking him! I think we shouldn't give him any more medicine. Maybe his hoof won't get infected anyhow. I'd rather him be lame than hate me, or maybe hurt someone."

The other girls nodded their heads when she was finished.

"I don't think Zipper wants to hurt anyone," Kendra said. "Normally he's a really nice horse. Now he's just too scared to think clearly."

"You shouldn't quit giving him medicine," Megan said. "My mom says a hoof abscess is really serious. If Zipper is lame, you won't be able to ride him for months."

"I know," Ruth-Ann said. "But maybe his hoof won't get infected."

"But maybe it will," Kendra said. "What if he was lame forever?"

Next Megan read her suggestion to the group.

"Zipper is fighting back to defend himself. He thinks we can't poke him if he keeps us away. I think we need more people to help us. Maybe my dad can come over. Or else we could take Zipper over to my place. My dad has a narrow pen called a chute where we could treat Zipper. Then he couldn't kick or hurt anyone when he gets his shots."

"That's an idea," Ruth-Ann said slowly. "But I'm afraid that Zipper will hurt himself if he struggles in the chute. And I think it's going to take a lot of people to force Zipper to stand still. After all, it took two grown-up nurses to hold down Mikey, and he's much smaller than Zipper."

"And I don't know if Mr. and Mrs. Lewis even want Zipper over there," Kendra said. "It's hard work treating a sick animal."

"And he needs that medicine every day," Ruth-Ann said. "He's probably going to behave worse and worse."

Last, Kendra read her suggestion. It was very short.

"Phone Trish and tell her the problem. Maybe she can help us."

"Why didn't I think of that?" Ruth-Ann asked. She knew Trish was good at solving problems.

Megan nodded her head. "OK," she said. "We should phone Trish. But I don't think anyone's going to solve this problem very easily. Even Trish and the R2R Club."

Trish's
Idea

"Hi, everyone," Trish called as she arrived at the Chow place the next afternoon. "How are my three pony girls doing?" Megan and Kendra began to visit with Trish while Ruth-Ann climbed over the corral fence to catch Zipper.

The little Paint seemed relaxed when Ruth-Ann haltered him. But his head rose and his ears began to flick back and forth when Ruth-Ann led him toward Trish.

"This is where Zipper got his shots yesterday," Ruth-Ann said. Zipper snorted and pranced backward a step.

"Horses have excellent memories," Trish said. She backed up a safe distance and then sat down in the grass with her back leaning against the wooden corral.

Zipper looked at Trish and seemed to recognize that she was not going to be a threat to him down there. He relaxed again and allowed Ruth-Ann to tie him to the post and brush him.

Trish began to tell a story from her spot in the grass. "Many years ago I had a bay mare named Rocket," Trish said. "One day an old tree fell on my electric fence and knocked the wire onto the ground. Rocket tried to walk over the electric fence and her legs got tangled. She was shocked several times before freeing herself."

"I've touched electric fences before," Ruth-Ann said with a shiver. "It really hurts!"

"This electric fence was operated by a solar panel," Trish said. "So it wasn't as powerful as many electric fences. But it scared Rocket so badly that for the rest of her life she wouldn't walk into that area without acting crazy. Even when the electric fence was gone, you couldn't ride her there. She remembered the bad experience."

Ruth-Ann put down her curry-comb and turned to Trish. "What can we do?" she asked. "I don't want Zipper to be scared forever! He's my friend, but that medicine is going to make him hate me."

Trish sighed. "Do you remember what I said about Tyler?"

"Tyler?" Ruth-Ann asked.

"Tyler Anderson," Megan said. "My sister's boyfriend. Remember? The guy who fell off Zipper?"

"Oh," Ruth-Ann said. "That Tyler."

"Yes, that Tyler," Trish said. "Remember how angry he was yesterday?"

"How can I forget?"

"I told you that sometimes people act strangely when they're afraid," Trish said. "Tyler really wasn't angry at us. He was scared."

"He could have fooled me," Ruth-Ann said.

"I talked to Tyler last night," Trish continued. "He isn't mad anymore. In fact, I think I persuaded him to come over to my place and meet my horses. I want to show him that horses aren't dangerous."

"Now you're pulling my leg!" Megan said. "Mandy told me that Tyler decided he wasn't ever going to come near a horse again!"

"I'm not even near your leg!" Trish said, laughing. "So I guess I didn't pull it. But I am trying to make a point about how people and animals can act when they're afraid. Zipper is scared of the needles. He's acting totally different than normal because he doesn't trust us."

"Can't we just stop giving him the medicine?" Ruth-Ann asked.

"I think Zipper needs medication," Trish said.

"But—"

"Let's phone Dr. Bob," Trish said. "I know that there are long-acting antibiotics that Zipper could have. That would mean that we wouldn't have to poke him every day, but maybe only every three days."

"That would be a bit better," Kendra said.

"Would he still need three shots at a time?" Ruth-Ann asked.

"Yes," Trish said. "But there are some types of antibiotics that horses can take by mouth. Maybe that would work for Zipper instead of needles."

"I don't think Zipper's going to want to drink medicine," Ruth-Ann said.

"Or take a big pill," Megan agreed.

"Horse medicine is often a powder," Trish said. "You mix it in their grain and hope they eat it. Since Zipper always thinks he's hungry, he may not mind the taste that much. At least it would be worth a try."

"Zipper normally eats everything," Kendra said.

"He likes red licorice," Ruth-Ann said. "And gumdrops."

"He likes most candy," Megan agreed.

"But not the really sour ones," Ruth-Ann said. "Unless they're cherry flavored."

"Well," Trish said with a grin, "then he probably won't mind the taste of the medicine as long as he has grain mixed with it."

Ruth-Ann felt herself beginning to relax. "I'm sure my dad will take me back to the vet clinic for some different medicine," she said. "He hated giving the shots to Zipper as much as I did."

"And if we do have to give Zipper the shots," Trish continued, "there are ways we can do it that will make it less difficult. We can use a twitch, if we have to." (A twitch is applied to a horse's nose to distract him from something uncomfortable.) "The most important thing is to keep everyone around Zipper safe. And to keep him safe too."

"I still don't understand why Zipper acted so horrible with his shots," Ruth-Ann said. "I didn't expect it. Zipper's normally so calm and quiet."

"I've seen this many times before," Trish said. "Often the calmest horses can be the worst ones to treat. They usually cooperate because they're just naturally kind and pleasant, but they really haven't learned they *have* to do what people want. And then when something goes wrong, they can go through a period of bad behavior."

"That sounds like Zipper," Ruth-Ann said.

"Ruth-Ann," Trish said, "do you trust Jesus?"

"Sure I do!" Ruth-Ann said. "I'm a Christian, aren't I? All Christians trust Jesus."

Trish smiled. "All Christians *should* trust Jesus. But often we live really good lives and don't have our faith tested. Then when something bad comes along, we're in real shock. We see our problems, and because we haven't learned to trust God, we get angry, or afraid, or sad."

Trish stood up and dusted off the back of her pants. "Girls," she said. "Now is the time to decide to trust Jesus no matter what. Trust Him when things go well, and trust

Him when things seem to go wrong. If you do that, everything will end up good in the end. If Zipper was smart enough to understand that, he would be OK too. If he knew that he could really trust us no matter what, he wouldn't be so scared of his shots. He still wouldn't like them, but he wouldn't have to struggle and fight."

A New Lesson

Ruth-Ann gently pulled on Zipper's reins and brought him to a halt. She patted the little Paint's sweaty neck and smiled.

The Ready to Ride Club had just finished a riding lesson with Trish. All three girls were learning to jump. At first Trish had started them walking and trotting over a series of ground poles. Then they used bricks to raise the poles a few inches high and trotted over them too.

Ruth-Ann had jumped Zipper over an actual jump. It was only knee high, but it had seemed gigantic to Ruth-Ann. Huge. Monstrous. Massive.

Zipper had jumped it without even blinking.

"Zipper jumps with very good style," Trish said, coming over to the pair. "He brought up his knees straight and square, and he didn't drag his back legs."

"I felt like I was going to fall off," Ruth-Ann said. Her face was covered with an enormous grin. "But it was fun!"

"Well, you have lots of practice to do," Trish said. "I'll be back next week, and we'll do some more work. Until then I don't want you to jump alone. Keep working on your basic ring work, and you can go over ground poles too. But no real jumping, OK?"

"OK," Ruth-Ann said with a nod. She swung out of the saddle and slid down to stand beside her little Paint. She traced the odd-shaped lobster claw patch down his shoulder and then looked at his leg.

Trish seemed to know what the girl was thinking. "I'm glad Zipper took that powder medicine so well," she said. "He didn't have any lameness at all, did he?"

Ruth-Ann reached over and gave Zipper's neck a hug. "No," she said. "He's been totally fine. I'm so glad things worked out OK for my little Zippitty Do Dah."

Trish smiled and turned to go. "I better keep moving," she called to the girls. "I have someone coming for a riding lesson at my place in half an hour."

"Have fun," Megan called. She waved from the back of Blondie's wide back.

"I will," Trish said. "After all, it will be Tyler's first real riding lesson."

"Tyler?"

"Tyler Anderson?" Megan exclaimed.

"I told you," Trish said. "You never know what God has in store for you, if you just trust and follow Him. Now remember that. And keep practicing your riding. Next week we're going to start posting the trot without stirrups. It will build up leg muscles and improve your balance."

The Ready to Ride Club members looked at each other and groaned.

When Ruth-Ann unsaddled Zipper, she closed her eyes for a moment and began to pray. The last few weeks had been full of adventures. Some had been good, and some had been down-right horrible.

Dear God, Ruth-Ann prayed quietly. *Help me trust You all the time. Even when things don't seem as good as normal. And thank you for my horse. My little Zippitty Do Dah. Amen.*

Words of Advice About Safety With Ponies

Do you have a horse or pony of your own?

I am fortunate enough to own four Paint horses and one miniature pony. The horses' names are Jesse, Chevy, Austin, and Magnum, and the pony's name is Honey. Jesse is my favorite, and he looks just like Zipper. He is a sorrel and even has a bald face, and a lobster shaped claw-mark on his side!

Horses and ponies are wonderful, but they can be dangerous at times. Anytime you work with a thousand-pound animal, there will be chances to get hurt. Likewise, any hockey player, snowboarder, motorcyclist, or soccer player can be hurt practicing their sport too!

All new riders should learn about horses from an experienced adult. If your parents don't know how to ride properly, you'll need lessons from a trainer, or you'll need to attend a Pony Club or 4-H.

Here are a few safety rules that everyone should follow when riding their pony.

1. Always wear an approved riding helmet. A bike helmet may be better than nothing, but it doesn't cover your head as well as a real riding helmet.

2. Always ride with footwear that has a heel (such as cowboy boots) so your foot can't get stuck in the stirrup.

3. Beginner riders need to start on the right horse. It doesn't matter if the horse is big or small, sorrel or gray, a mare or a gelding. What matters is that the animal is well trained, quiet, and sensible. An older horse or pony is often best because they will be experienced.

4. Practice the riding basics in a safe location such as a riding ring until you know what your horse will do under all circumstances before riding in the open.

5. Don't take foolish chances. If your horse is acting silly when you're leading him, he'll probably act silly when you start riding. Get an adult to help you.

6. Keep your bridle, saddle, and halter in good condition, and make sure you put them on correctly and tight enough so they won't fall off when you least expect it.

7. Before each ride you should get a feel for your horse's temperament for the day. On windy or cold days most horses will be more jumpy than usual. If you feel your horse is going to misbehave, do groundwork first so your horse starts listening to you. Longe your horse, lead him from the ground, work in an enclosed area—do whatever it takes to keep you safe and your horse obedient.

Ask God to help you when you ride. You need God in all your activities, every single day, not just at church! He cares about everything you do, and He wants the best for you.

I hope you enjoy my Ready to Ride books. I enjoyed writing them for you.

Happy trails!
Heather Grovet

Want more horse stories? You'll enjoy these also.

The Sonrise Farm Series

Based on true stories, *Katy Pistole's* Sonrise Farm series about Jenny Thomas and her Palomino mare, Sunny, teaches children about horses and God's redeeming grace. (ages 11–13) Paperback, 128 pages each. US$7.99 each.

Book 1 **The Palomino**
Jenny Thomas has her heart set on one thing—a golden Palomino all her own. Her daring rescue of an abused horse at an auction begins an enduring friendship with Sunny. 0-8163-1863-8

Book 2 **Stolen Gold**
Book two in the series finds Sunny in the clutches of an abusive former owner who wants to collect insurance money on the Palomino and her colt. 0-8163-1882-4

Book 3 **Flying High**
A record-breaking jump, Sunny's reputation, and Jenny's relationship with God are all at stake when Jenny and her Palomino champion come face to face with their old enemy. 0-8163-1942-1

Book 4 **Morning Glory**
Sunny's foal is born, but an evil plan from Jenny's old enemy, Vanessa DuBois, threatens all of them. But God has a plan to restore their lives. 0-8163-2036-5

Order from your ABC by calling **1-800-765-6955**, or get online and shop our virtual store at **http://www.Adventist BookCenter.com**.
- Read a chapter from your favorite book
- Order online
- Sign up for e-mail notices on new products

Prices subject to change without notice.